Scholastic's
The Magic School Bus

GOES UPSTREAM
A Book About Salmon Migration

SCHOLASTIC INC.
New York   Toronto   London   Auckland   Sydney

From an episode of the animated TV series
produced by Scholastic Productions, Inc.
Based on *The Magic School Bus* books
written by Joanna Cole and illustrated by Bruce Degen

TV tie-in adaptation by Nancy E. Krulik and illustrated by Nancy Stevenson.
TV script written by Ronnie Krauss.

ISBN 0-590-92232-7

12 11 10 9 8 7 6 5 4 3   7 8 9/9 0 1 2/0

Printed in the U.S.A.   23

First Scholastic printing, June 1997

It was time for our school's annual Fish Fry Picnic. Each class was assigned a food to bring. Most classes went on field trips to local farms to get their food.

But not Ms. Frizzle's class!

Our class does things a little differently! We like to try new things. Ask questions. Get messy. Or, in this case, get wet. We were out on the Magic School bus-boat, fishing for salmon in the middle of the ocean.

Unfortunately, there weren't any salmon around.

I don't get it. Last spring there were so many salmon here you wouldn't believe it. My Uncle Brian and I saw tons of them!

Then where are they now?

We were getting nervous. If we didn't catch anything, the Fish Fry would be ruined!

"You promised fish, Ralphie, when you organized the picnic and the baseball game," Wanda insisted.

Ralphie's face turned red. "I know, I know," he answered. "Let's stick it out a little longer. We have to catch something."

Suddenly, Ralphie felt a big tug on his fishing line!

Ralphie had a big one on his line. It took all of us to pull it in. We tugged really hard. The bus-boat rocked back and forth. Water splashed high in the air. Finally we heard a thud. We'd done it! We'd pulled in a giant . . .

"I was just testing out our new fearsomely fast flippers," Ms. Frizzle explained. "And I have to say, they're fin-tastic!"

Ralphie sighed. "I wish I could say the same thing about the fishing, Ms. Frizzle," he said. "But you're the only thing we've caught all day."

"Oh dear!" Ms. Frizzle replied. "Don't tell me there's a salmon famine when you've promised to feed the whole school fish?!"

Wait a minute. We're supposed to *look* for salmon, not become one!

Ms. Frizzle got that *time-for-a-field-trip* look in her eye. We followed her into the cabin of the Magic School bus-boat.

"Are you taking us home, Ms. Frizzle?" Ralphie asked.

"Let me put it this way, Ralphie. When your salmon have got up and gone, it's time to get up and go!" Ms. Frizzle exclaimed. "Hit it, Liz!"

Liz pulled down a lever on the dashboard. The bus-boat spun around in the open sea. Its headlights bulged like giant eyes. It grew fins and a tail! Obviously, the bus wasn't going back to school just yet.

But where was it going?!

"Actually, class, the bus hasn't turned into a real salmon," Ms. Frizzle told us as she popped a disk into a computer on the dashboard. "But with this new Microbus software, it will think it has! This disk programs the bus to have a brain and memory just like a salmon. It will go wherever your salmon went, Ralphie."

There were computer monitors all over the bus. "Those are Microbus windows," Ms. Frizzle explained. "They let us see what the bus is thinking."

The bus swam along. We all got up and looked at the different Microbus windows screens. Keesha sniffed at the smell station. "Don't you just love that salty-ocean smell!" she said.

Carlos and Dorothy Ann watched the screen at the sight station. That way they could see what the bus was seeing. Suddenly, a school of smaller fish appeared on the screen. The bus had spotted lunch! It opened its mouth wide to catch the fish.

Phoebe and Ralphie watched the screen at the taste station. As the bus swallowed the fish, a picture of small fish appeared on the screen.

"Over here, Ms. Frizzle," Arnold called as he watched a wavy line move across his screen. "Something weird is happening."

"That's a pressure sensor," Ms. Frizzle explained. "It runs in a line along each side of the salmon-bus. The lines can feel even the tiniest movement in the water. That way the salmon can sense what it can't see with its eyes."

Ralphie looked worried. "Like things that might *eat* us?" he asked nervously.

Suddenly we spotted a huge fish with rows and rows of sharp teeth. It was heading right for us!

"Excuse me, Ms. Frizzle, but we're outta here!" Ralphie cried. He raced to the dashboard, turned the steering wheel, and pressed his foot against the gas pedal.

Nothing happened.

"The gas pedal doesn't work and the steering wheel won't turn," Ralphie said.

"Of course not, Ralphie," Ms. Frizzle replied. "We're not in control anymore. The bus is. It's thinking like a salmon!"

"We're fin-ished," Carlos declared.

Come on, even a salmon has to take chances, make mistakes, and get . . .

EATEN!!!

The Magic School salmon-bus darted down deep into the ocean. It picked up speed and swam off. Phew! We'd just missed being lunch for a shark!

And speaking of lunch, Dorothy Ann spotted another school of tiny fish. "Hey, guys, it's feeding time again," she announced.

But this time the bus didn't stop for a snack. Instead, it joined up with a group of other salmon and kept on swimming.

Dorothy Ann flipped the pages of her notebook. "Wait a minute," she said. "According to my research, when a salmon loses its appetite, starts swimming hard in one direction, and is joined by other salmon all going the same way, it's migrating!"

"You mean like birds in the fall?" Keesha asked.

"It says here that some animals that migrate travel thousands of miles!" Dorothy Ann continued. "And it can take months."

"Which means we might make it back in time for our *senior* picnic," Carlos added.

Ralphie jumped up excitedly. "I have a plan!" he said. "We'll just go outside and turn the bus around!"

Ms. Frizzle nodded and walked across the bus to a closet. She pulled out four pairs of bright orange flippers. "Don't go without your flippers," she said. "They might come in handy."

We watched through the windows as Ralphie, Wanda, Carlos, and Keesha swam out into the water. The salmon seemed really big to them. But the salmon hadn't grown. We'd all shrunk when the bus became a salmon!

"I feel like a real shrimp," Carlos joked.

"Quit complaining! Let's stop this salmon-bus, so we can go home," Ralphie said.

The kids swam ahead of the bus as quickly as they could. They stopped in a place that the bus would have to pass. "Okay now, hold hands!" Ralphie ordered. They joined hands and waited for the bus to stop.

But the bus didn't stop.

The bus was heading right for Ralphie, Wanda, Carlos, and Keesha! We thought they were done for!

But just as the bus was about to flatten them, it dived down deep into the water and swam beneath them.

Wanda watched as the bus swam off. "Now what are we going to do?" she asked Ralphie.

"There's only one thing *to* do," Ralphie answered. "Catch the bus, and stop it."

While Ralphie was outside chasing the bus, we were inside trying to stop it. But no matter what buttons we pushed, the bus kept swimming.

"Where are we heading?" Tim asked.

"I don't know," Arnold replied from the taste station, "but according to the bus, the water's getting less salty. It's changing over to fresh water."

"But saltwater fish die in fresh water!" Dorothy Ann cried out.

Follow that fish-bus!

Ms. Frizzle did not look nervous. (Then again, she never does.) "Salmon are amazing creatures that can switch safely from being saltwater fish to freshwater fish. A perfect flip-flop," she explained.

Tim glanced through a porthole. "It looks like they go through other changes, too," he said as a school of salmon swam by. The male salmon had grown humps on their backs and had hooked jaws. The females had big, puffed-up bellies.

Suddenly the salmon-bus's belly puffed up, too. Now we knew which type of salmon the bus was — a female!

The bus was slowing down, which made it easier for Ralphie, Wanda, Carlos, and Keesha to catch it. "We're gaining on 'em, partners," Ralphie called as he rode along on his trusty salmon. "Let's corral that bus! WAAAAHOOO!"

But the bus had already stopped. It was caught in a big salmon traffic jam in the bay at the mouth of the river. "It's as if we're waiting for something," Tim said.

"Right as rain," Ms. Frizzle replied. "The river is low and there's not much water coming down."

"River?" Carlos asked. "You mean we swam all the way from out in the ocean to a river? For what?"

"Maybe the salmon are waiting for the river to rise," Phoebe said. Just then, it started to rain.

Suddenly a seal leaped into the water. It was hungry for salmon. What if the seal grabbed some small swimming kids or a salmon-shaped bus instead?

Outside, Ralphie, Wanda, Carlos, and Keesha swam for cover. Inside the bus, we watched as the seal came closer and closer. Then the seal grabbed a nearby salmon and darted off. *Whew!*

Phoebe sniffed at the air. "What is that smell?" she asked. "It reminds me of something, somewhere. If I were a fish, I'd follow that smell anywhere."

"I don't recognize it," Arnold said. "But I think the bus does."

Just then we heard a loud banging on the side of the bus. Ralphie, Keesha, Wanda, and Carlos wanted us to let them in. But before Liz could open the hatch for them, the bus swam forward. It was following that smell.

Phoebe was right. We were waiting for the river to rise. We started heading upstream — and fast! But Ralphie really wanted to stop the bus so we could all head home. This time, he had a plan that couldn't miss! Ralphie climbed up on a dam that the salmon would have to jump over. Carlos, Keesha, and Wanda followed close behind. They piled twigs and branches on top of the dam to make it higher.

"This plan is foolproof," Ralphie said as he laid down some more branches. "The bus will never make it over the dam."

The bus swam up to the dam. It leaped high up into the air. But not high enough. The bus fell backwards into the water.

"I knew it would work," Ralphie cheered.

Wanda nodded. But the bus really did seem determined. It had left a good feeding place in the ocean, dived beneath a shark, and successfully avoided a seal! Plus, it had changed into a freshwater fish so it could swim upriver! Had Ralphie really found a way to outsmart the bus?

The bus and a fellow salmon thrust their tails hard into the water. *SPLASH!* A huge wave of fresh water smacked Ralphie in the face. Together with the real salmon, we soared over the dam.

We stopped in a tiny little stream. The smell in the bus got really strong.

The Magic School salmon-bus began digging a hole, just like all of the other females.

"I can't believe it!" Dorothy Ann exclaimed. "We came all this way just to dig a hole?"

"Not just any hole, Dorothy Ann. You'll see," Ms. Frizzle replied mysteriously.

Ralphie, Wanda, Keesha, and Carlos banged on the hatch of the bus. "We're finally done, Ms. Frizzle," Ralphie said. "The bus has migrated. Can we please go home now?"

"Sure thing, Ralphie," Ms. Frizzle agreed. "After one more *eggs*-perience!"

A chute opened on the side of the bus. But instead of letting Ralphie, Keesha, Carlos, and Wanda in . . . it let the rest of us out!

We finally knew why female salmon migrate — to find a place to lay their eggs. What we couldn't figure out was why the males migrated. So we did what Ms. Frizzle's always telling us to do. We asked questions.

"Excuse me, sir," Carlos asked a male salmon. "We were wondering — any particular reason why you're here?"

The salmon didn't answer. He sprayed us with something that looked a little cloudy in the water.

There's your answer, Carlos.

What? He's some kind of car wash?

"The eggs have to be fertilized by the males before they can grow and hatch," Ms. Frizzle explained.

Suddenly the bus began to use its tail to cover us with gravel.

"The bus is burying us alive!" Wanda cried out.

"It must be okay — the real salmon are burying their eggs, too," Tim assured her.

Ms. Frizzle hit a green switch. "I'm going to speed things up a bit. It's time to hatch!" she announced.

Before long, we hatched out of the eggs. We were born! Being little salmon was really great! We were safe in our shallow stream, and there was plenty of food.

"How did the salmon know about this place?" Ralphie asked.

"The bus kept smelling a place far away," Tim began.

"And the smell got stronger as we got closer!" Dorothy Ann added.

"I think we *smelled* our way here," Arnold said.

We'd figured it out. To salmon, every stream has its own smell. Salmon remember the exact scent of the stream where they were born. They just follow the smell home!

We knew that once the salmon got a little bigger, they'd have to migrate back to the ocean, where there was plenty of food and room to grow. Luckily, we didn't have to migrate again. Ms. Frizzle opened a hatch on the bus. We swam in and became kids again. The Friz pushed another button and the bus changed from a salmon to a goose! We flew home in style!

The other classes were just about to give up on us when we arrived at the Fish Fry. "We're here!" Ralphie called. "With potato fish fries for all!"

The other kids looked at him strangely. "We found salmon," Ralphie explained. "But they were making a journey so incredible, we decided to let them be!"

Letters from Our Readers

Dear Editor,
I have a question to ask. Do salmon really make that long migration in one day? Isn't the ocean really far from the stream?
Signed,
Maureen Corps

Dear Maureen,
You're right. There's no way salmon could make the journey in just one day. It really takes about 6 months. But hey, we only have 32 pages in this book, so we crammed all of their adventures into one day.
—The Editor

Dear Editor,
Salmon are real superheroes. They swim upriver against strong currents! They leap tall dams in a single bound. They'll do almost anything to get home. It seems as though no enemy is too tough for them. Salmon aren't even afraid of kryptonite!
Have you ever considered making comic books about Super Salmon?
Signed,
Clark K.

Dear Clark,
Salmon certainly are super. But don't fool yourself. They can fall victim to plenty of enemies, including bears, birds, pollution, and fishermen. In fact, more salmon die than live during migration. Still, every year enough salmon reach their destination to get the big payoff in the end. We'll take your idea into consideration.
—The Editor

From the Desk of Ms. Frizzle

Dear Kids, Parents, and Teachers:

Did you know that salmon aren't the only fish that make amazing migrations to places where they can safely hatch and raise their young?

Take the American eel, for instance. It takes the opposite route from the salmon. The eel breeds in the ocean but spends most of its life in freshwater streams. Adult eels from all over North America and Europe swim to one place in the Sargasso Sea (that's right near Bermuda). When they get there, they lay their eggs and die. The tiny eel larvae drift about in the Gulf Stream. Eventually they reach the river mouths and start their upstream migration. Eels can live for 6 to 12 years in fresh water before they begin their long trip back to the Sargasso Sea, where they will have ample room and food to live as adult eels.

Some fish, like albacore tuna, migrate within different parts of the ocean. The adults leave their eating grounds and swim against ocean currents to the place where they lay and fertilize their tiny tuna eggs. The helpless young are carried by the ocean currents to good feeding grounds. As the young grow and get stronger, they swim back to the adult feeding grounds their parents left behind. This tuna migration pattern forms a sort of triangle.

Happy traveling!

Ms. Frizzle